W9-BYW-719

BAD

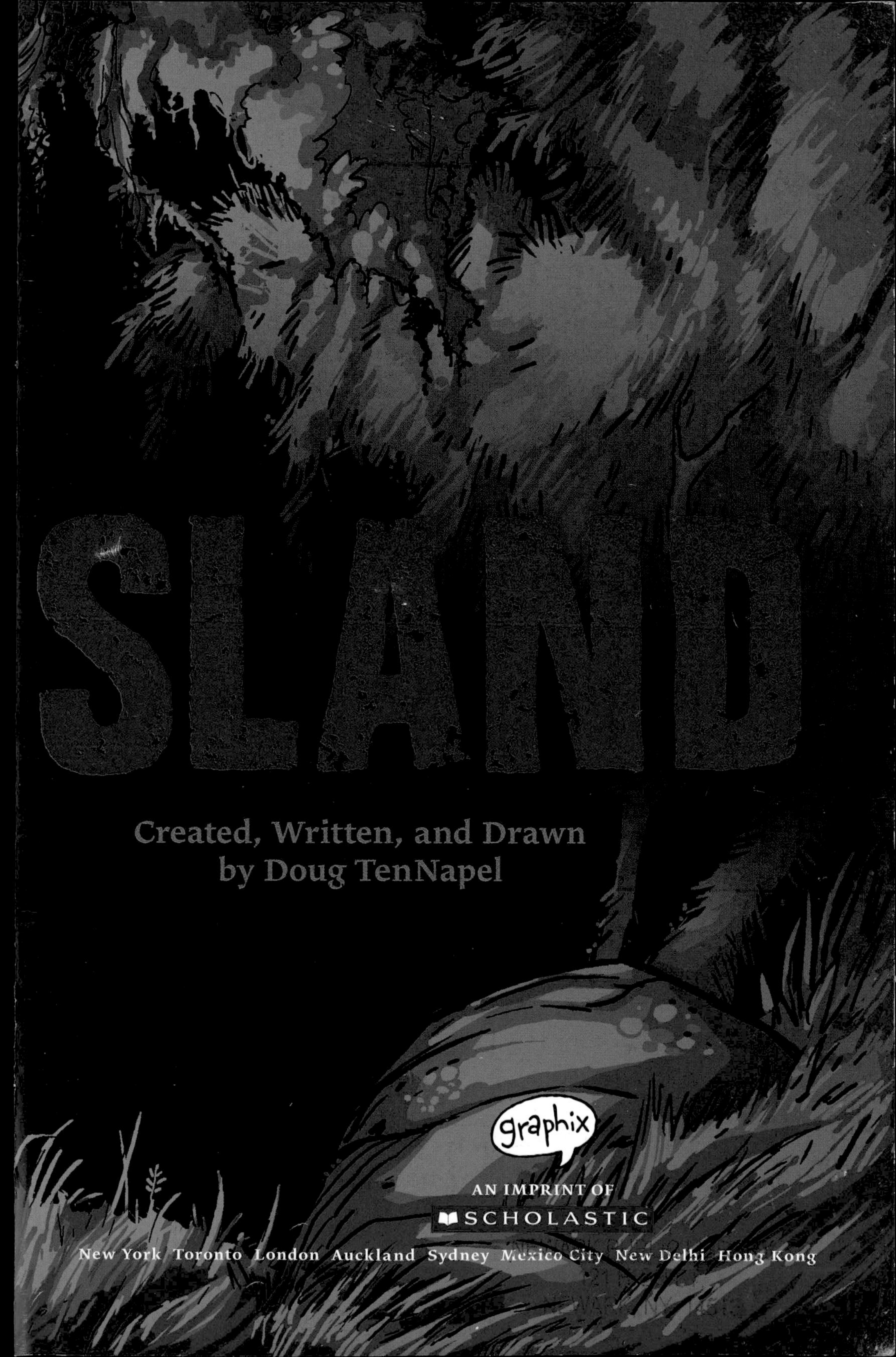

SLAND

Created, Written, and Drawn
by Doug TenNapel

graphix

AN IMPRINT OF
SCHOLASTIC

New York Toronto London Auckland Sydney Mexico City New Delhi Hong Kong

This book is dedicated to Ray Harryhausen.

Credits:

Lead Colorists: Katherine Garner and Josh Kenfield

Color Assistance by Ryan Agadoni, Wesley Scoggins, Dirk Erik Schulz, William Crawford, Ethan Nicolle, Phil Falco, Sean Farbolin, Matt Burbridge, Jared Morgan, and Matt Doering

Book Design by Phil Falco

Edited by Adam Rau and David Saylor

Creative Director: David Saylor

Special thanks to:

My beloved Angie, Ahmi, Edward, Olivia, Johnny, Michael Beckner, Ethan Nicolle, David Saylor, Phil Falco, Adam Rau, Eddie Gamarra, the Chestertonians, Brad Bird, John Williams, and the Neverhood crew, for teaching me that worlds should also be puzzles.

This book was inked using Manga Studio Ex 4.

Copyright © 2011 by Doug TenNapel

All rights reserved. Published by Graphix, an imprint of Scholastic Inc., *Publishers since 1920*. SCHOLASTIC, GRAPHIX, and associated logos are trademarks and/or registered trademarks of Scholastic Inc.

No part of this publication may be reproduced, stored in a retrieval system, or transmitted in any form or by any means, electronic, mechanical, photocopying, recording, or otherwise, without written permission of the publisher. For information regarding permission, write to Scholastic Inc., Attention: Permissions Department, 557 Broadway, New York, NY 10012.

Library of Congress Cataloging-in-Publication Data Available

ISBN 978-0-545-31479-4 (hardcover)
ISBN 978-0-545-31480-0 (paperback)

10 9 8 7 6 5 4 3 2 1   11 12 13 14 15

Printed in Singapore 46

First edition, August 2011

ANOTHER WORLD,
ANOTHER TIME...

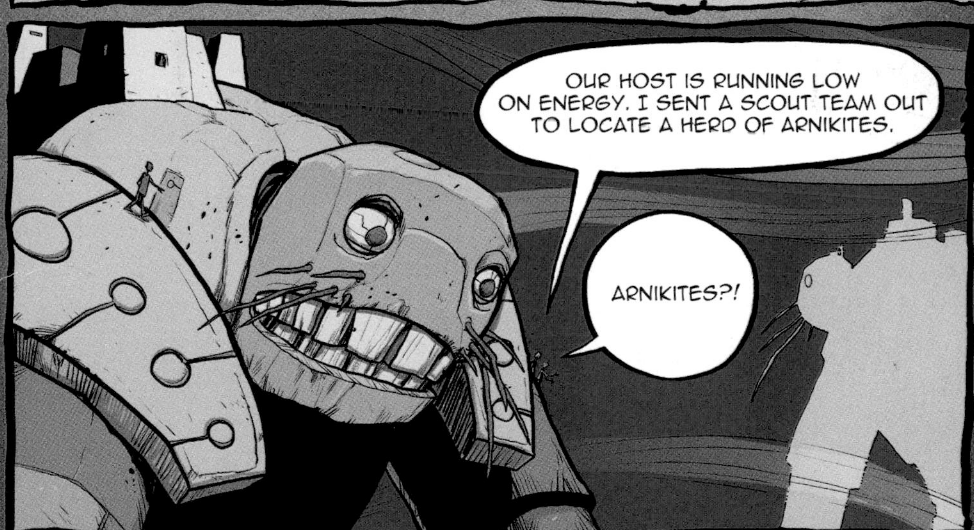
OUR HOST IS RUNNING LOW ON ENERGY. I SENT A SCOUT TEAM OUT TO LOCATE A HERD OF ARNIKITES.
ARNIKITES?!

THAT IS NO WAY TO CELEBRATE THE ONE-HUNDRED-YEAR ANNIVERSARY OF OUR LIBERATION! THEY GAVE US OUR FREEDOM! THEY DESERVE BETTER THAN A HERD OF SCRAWNY ARNIKITES!

I WILL SET A COURSE THAT WILL GET US TO THE ENERGY POOLS OF MURCURON! TONIGHT, OUR GIANT WILL FEAST ON THE BEST WE HAVE TO OFFER!
GOOD IDEA!

FSSSSSS

THAT SHOULD DO IT!
CHUNK
WHAT ARE THOSE THINGS COMING DOWN FROM THE SKY?

OH, NO! THEY HAVE RETURNED!

KRAAA
REVENGE!
WE MUST BRING THE DEFENSES UP BEFORE THEY ARRIVE!
THERE'S NO TIME! THEY ARE UPON US!

ALL INHABITANTS PREPARE FOR IMPACT!

BASH

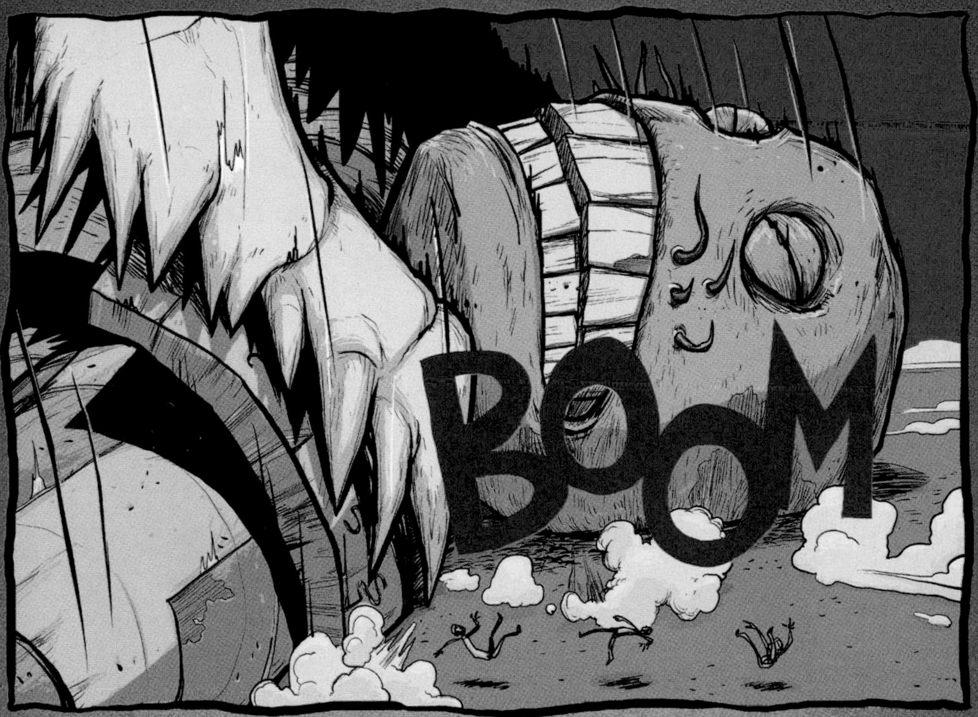
BOOM

HOLD ON TIGHT!
WE MUST RETRIEVE THE BATTLE-ARMOR PROGRAM!

EVACUATE! THEY HAVE COME BACK!

FLIP

HURRY UP WITH THAT BATTLE-ARMOR PROGRAM!

WE'RE LOOKING! BUT THE ACTIVATOR LIBRARY IS A MESS!
NOPE, NOT THIS ONE. THIS ONE IS NOT IT, EITHER!

I FOUND IT!

CHONK

BVARRRR
BVVVT
NOW WE FIGHT!

SPOW
SPOW
YOU WILL NOT ENSLAVE THESE PEOPLE AGAIN!
SPOW

PING
BOMM
PLAM

BIM
BIM
BIM
BIM
FRAAAA
BIM

...PRESENT DAY.
REESE! I NEED YOUR HELP LOADING THE CAR!

TELL YOUR FRIENDS YOU'VE GOTTA GO.

AW, DAD.

HOLD TIGHT, GUYS.

HOW AM I GONNA GET OUT OF THIS STUPID TRIP?

DAD, HAVE YOU SEEN PICKLES?
NOT NOW, JANIE.

KAREN, I PACKED THE ICE CHEST. IF YOU NEED TO ADD ANYTHING, COULD YOU HURRY UP SO I CAN POUR THE ICE OVER EVERYTHING?
NOT NOW, LYLE. I HAVE TO ADJUST THIS DRIP SYSTEM FIRST.
MOM WOULDN'T HAVE TO AUTOMATE THE WATERING IF I JUST STAYED HOME AND WATERED THE PLANTS BY HAND!

NOT NOW, SON.
REESE, HAVE *YOU* SEEN PICKLES?
NOT NOW, INFANT.

BUT, DAD, JUSTIN'S PARENTS LET HIM STAY AT HOME ALONE FOR A WHOLE WEEKEND AND HE'S SIX MONTHS YOUNGER THAN ME!
REESE, I DON'T TRUST YOU. THERE, I SAID IT. YOU HAPPY NOW?
PUT A STOP ON THE MAIL. CHECK.

SET DIGITAL TELEVISION TO RECORD SHOWS. CHECK!

STUPID!

MOM! I CAN'T FIND PICKLES AND NOBODY WILL HELP!
JANIE, IF I DON'T GET THIS WATERING SYSTEM SET UP RIGHT, I'M GOING TO HAVE AN EXPENSIVE-BUT-DEAD ORCHID ON MY HANDS.

BUT PICKLES COULD BE--
I'M TRYING TO BE SENSITIVE TO YOUR NEEDS, BUT THIS ORCHID IS A *LA PEDRENA*. THAT'S PERUVIAN FOR "WORTH MORE THAN PICKLES."

THAT SHOULD DO IT. IF THIS STUPID BOAT TRIP KILLS MY BABY, I'M NEVER GOING TO TRAVEL AGAIN!
NOW CAN YOU HELP ME?

SORRY, SWEETIE. I HAVE TO REPACK AN ICE CHEST.
CAN YOU HELP ME WHEN YOU'RE DONE? HOW LONG CAN IT TAKE TO REPACK AN ICE CHEST?

...A LONG TIME. YOUR FATHER PACKED IT.
KISS
BUT, MOM--

RIP
RIP
RIP
RIP

FIRST AID KIT... CHECK. FISHING GEAR...CHECK. ICE CHEST...
YOU EVER HEAR OF A THING CALLED VEGETABLES? THEY DO EXIST, YOU KNOW!

HEY, I ALREADY PACKED THAT ICE CHEST JUST FINE! THEN YOU COME ALONG AND EDIT MY SELECTIONS!
LYLE, FILLING AN ICE CHEST WITH THE FIRST FIVE KINDS OF MEAT YOU FIND IS NOT PACKING NUTRI-TIOUS MEALS FOR THE FAMILY!
I THOUGHT WE'D CELEBRATE OUR TRIP BY HAVING FUN FOOD. MEAT PRODUCTS WITH A THREE-HUNDRED-YEAR SHELF LIFE ARE A GOOD START!
WAAAAAAH
CAN YOU PLEASE TAKE CARE OF THAT?
I'M ON IT.
DADDEEEEEE!
DADDY'S RIGHT HERE, JANIE!

AW, WHAT HAPPENED, SWEETHEART?
IT'S PICKLES! HE'S GONE! WE CAN'T LEAVE UNTIL HE'S FOUND! HE-HE-HE'S PROBABLY REALLY SCARED!

WHERE DID YOU LAST SEE HIM? DID YOU LEAVE HIS CASE OPEN?

GYAAA-AAAAA!!
PICKLES!

JANIE, GET THIS SNAKE OFF OF ME!

YESSS!

PICKLES, YOU CAME BACK TO ME! I KNEW YOU COULDN'T STAY AWAY FOREVER! YOU'RE MY BESTEST FRIEND!

I'M EXTREMELY HAPPY FOR YOU.

PICKLES WANTS A KISS, TOO!
I'M NOT KISSING THAT THING.

B-B-BUT HE L-LOVES YOU. JUST LIKE I LOVE YOU.

OKAY, KISSY-KISS.

BITE

GYAAAAAA

STUPID SNAKE!
LYLE, NEVER KISS A SNAKE.

HOLY CROW.
DANGER

OOF!

HUH?

MOM!
YES?

UH...

YOU'RE ALL GROWN UP!
I AM?

YOU ALREADY PACKED FOR THE BIG BOAT TRIP! NOW I DON'T HAVE TO BARK AT YOU TO DO IT!

Y-Y-YOU'RE WELCOME.

BUT I STILL DON'T UNDERSTAND WHY I HAVE TO GO. CAN'T YOU TALK TO HIM, MOM?
LOOK, REESE, NOBODY IS THRILLED ABOUT GOING ON THIS TRIP! JUST GO ALONG AND TRY TO MAKE THE BEST OF IT.

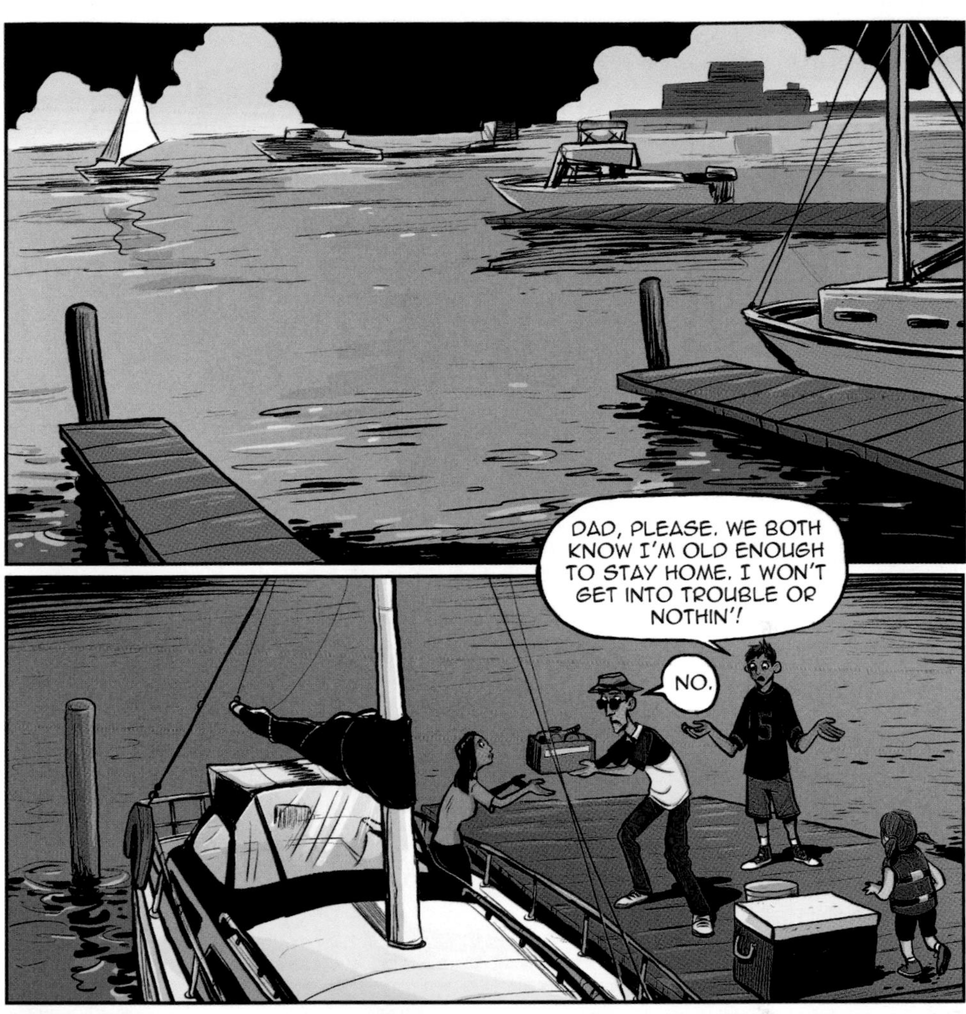
DAD, PLEASE. WE BOTH KNOW I'M OLD ENOUGH TO STAY HOME. I WON'T GET INTO TROUBLE OR NOTHIN'!
NO.

I'M JUST GOING TO FOOTBALL PRACTICE WITH THE GUYS!
WE NEED FAMILY TIME. I NEED TO GET US AWAY FROM THE BUSYNESS AND DISTRAC-TIONS.

...THIS BOAT TRIP IS THE DISTRACTION!

HEY! NOT SO TIGHT!
SORRY, JANIE...

I DON'T WANT YOU SLIPPING AROUND IN THERE!

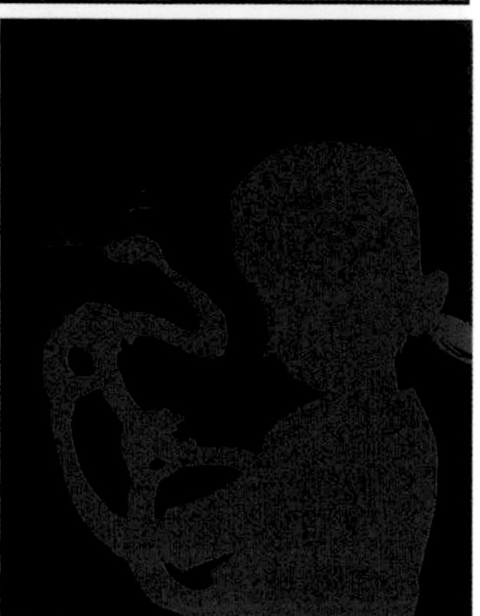

SHHHHH

LET'S GOOO! THE SEA CAN'T WAIT ANY LONGER!

WHY DO I HAVE TO GO? IT'S GOING TO BE TOTALLY LAME! WHY CAN'T YOU JUST BE A NORMAL DAD AND NEGLECT ME?
BECAUSE THEN YOU'D HAVE TOO MUCH FUN AND MY JOB AS YOUR PERSONAL JOY KILLER WOULD BE A FAILURE.
I DON'T GET WHAT'S SO BAD ABOUT SPENDING A LITTLE TIME WITH YOUR FAMILY!

CRACKK
EVERYONE, TIGHTEN YOUR LIFE VESTS!
253
SOMOS DOS

THE RADIO'S FRIED!

I'M SCARED, MOMMY!
DIDN'T YOU CHECK THE WEATHER REPORT BEFORE WE LEFT?

YEAH, IT SAID THAT TODAY WOULD BE SUNNY WITH PARTIAL CLOUDS!

DAD, THIS IS NUTS! IT'S COMING IN TOO FAST!

HOLD ON!

HOLD ON...TO EACH OTHER!

IS EVERYONE OKAY?

JANIE?!

JANIEEEEE!

WHERE ARE YOU?!

I DON'T KNOW WHAT TO DO! WHERE'S MY JANIE?

WAAAAAH

I'M ON MY WAY!

DADDEEEEEEEE!
WHAT HAPPENED?

ARE YOU OKAY? ARE YOU HURT, HONEY?
NOT ME...

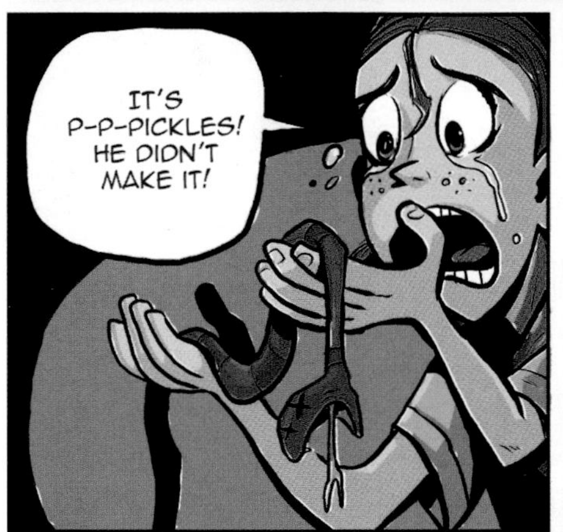
IT'S P-P-PICKLES! HE DIDN'T MAKE IT!

THE SNAKE DIED.
OH, THANK GOD IT'S JUST THE SNAKE!

DID PICKLES... DO YOU THINK HE WENT TO HEAVEN?
I DON'T KNOW, JANIE...

...BUT IF THERE IS A SNAKE HEAVEN I'M SURE PICKLES WILL BE THE FIRST ONE TO SLITHER THROUGH THAT DOOR.

GEEZ. NICE TRIP, DAD.

THE MAIN THING IS THAT WE'RE ALIVE AND TOGETHER. THAT'S HUGE!
BUT WHAT ARE WE GOING TO DO NOW?

FIRST, WE GET EVERYTHING OF VALUE OFF THE BOAT!

EASY DOES IT!
I'VE GOT IT. MY HULKING ARMS CAN HANDLE IT JUST FINE!

WHOA!
CREAKK

BASH

SPLASH

GREAT. WE'VE ONLY GOT ELEVEN MORE YEARS OF PAYMENTS ON THAT THING.
DON'T LOOK AT ME. I WANTED THE TIME-SHARE.

DON'T BE SCARED, PICKLES! AND DON'T BOTHER DAD IF YOU NEED HELP. IF ANYTHING HAPPENS, I'LL BE HERE FOR YOU!
HERE, LET ME GET THIS SIDE! I'LL PULL IT UP WHILE YOU PUSH!
UH! ARE YOU HELPING ME YET? BECAUSE I'M NOT FEELING IT IF YOU ARE!
CAN SOMEONE PLEASE GET A CLUE ABOUT WHICH WAY WE'RE GOING? WATCHING YOU TWO BICKER WHILE GOING IN CIRCLES MAKES ME FEEL LIKE WE'RE BACK HOME IN THE MINIVAN!

THIS IS THE FIRST TIME I'M SAD TO SEE AN ABSENCE OF TRASH. NO TRASH, NO PEOPLE.
WE'LL USE THE BOAT'S SAIL AS A TARP AND MAKE A LITTLE SHELTER RIGHT HERE! THEN WE CAN HAVE A LOOK AROUND.

I'M KIND OF WORRIED. WHAT ARE WE SUPPOSED TO DO OUT HERE IN THE MIDDLE OF NOWHERE?
SAME AS WE ALWAYS DO FOR THE KIDS...PRETEND LIKE WE KNOW WHAT WE'RE DOING.

FLINK
FLINK
FLINK

WHAT'S DAD SUPPOSED TO BE DOING?
...TRYING TO LOOK HELPLESS.

THANKS. YOU'RE A REAL BOOST TO MY SELF-CONFIDENCE.

HERE'S WHAT THEY USE TO START FIRES ON MY PLANET.

ZIP
PLINK
DANG.
ZIP
OUCH!

THIS TIME FOR SURE.

OH, MAN! OH, MAN!

DID WE SALVAGE THE FIRE EXTINGUISH-ER?

POOM

FSSSSSSS

ON A CLEAR NIGHT LIKE THIS, A FLARE CAN BE SEEN FROM MILES AWAY!

GREAT. NOW THE PIRATES WILL HAVE AN EASIER TIME FINDING US!
JANIE, WOULD YOU LIKE WATER OR A JUICE BOX?
SNAP

JUICE BOX.

I DON'T GET THE PLANTS ON THIS ISLAND.

WATCHA GOT THERE?
ON THE SURFACE THESE PLANTS LOOK JUST LIKE OUR PLANTS AT HOME.

BUT A CLOSER LOOK REVEALS THAT STRUC-TURALLY THEY AREN'T LIKE ANY PLANT I'VE EVER SEEN!

AH, MY LITTLE BOTANY MAJOR! PERHAPS YOU JUST DIS-COVERED A NEW SPECIES!
NOPE. THIS LOOKS EXACTLY LIKE CURRANT. BUT IT HAS NO ROOTS AND THE LEAVES DON'T APPEAR TO HAVE A PHOTOSYNTHETIC SYSTEM.
SOME-THING'S UP WITH THIS ISLAND, LYLE!

HUH. SO THERE ARE SOME WEIRD PLANTS. THAT CAN BE EXPECTED.
I DON'T LIKE IT.

SNIFF
SNIFF

GOOD MORNING, REESE!
SNIFF SNIFF SNIFF

I MADE YOU SOME CEREAL, FRUIT, HARD-BOILED EGGS, AND OKRA.
OKRA. WHY?

BECAUSE IT'S FROM OUR GARDEN. AND IT'S GOOD FOR YOU!
I DON'T CARE IF WE'RE SHIP-WRECKED, I'M NOT EATING THAT.

WAIT. WHO THE HECK MADE THOSE FOOT-PRINTS?
I DON'T KNOW.

WELL, WHO ELSE COULD BE ON THIS ISLAND?
THAT'S WHAT I INTEND TO FIND OUT.

HOLD ON A SEC. I GOTTA USE THE BUSHES.

OKAY, I'LL JUST TAKE PICKLES OUT FOR A LITTLE WALK.

THAT'S GROSS. YOU SHOULD BURY THAT DEAD SNAKE BEFORE IT STARTS TO STINK!

HIDING PLACE

WHO SAID THAT?
WHAT?
I DIDN'T SAY ANY-THING.

SOMEONE JUST SAID, "HIDING PLACE"!
SOMEONE ALSO DREW A SQUIGGLE ON THIS ROCK. GREAT! THIS ISLAND DOESN'T HAVE FLUSHING TOILETS BUT IT HAS TAGGERS.

REESE, I'M GETTING SCARED AND SO IS PICKLES!

COME ON. WE'D BETTER CATCH UP TO MOM AND DAD BEFORE THEY GET LOST!

SUDDENLY, I'M NOT SO THIRSTY ANYMORE.
HERE'S SOME FOR YOU, TOO, PICKLES! WOW! YOU'RE THIRSTY!

UH!

THIS'LL BE MY NEW WALKING STICK!

DANG. IT'S A LITTLE LONG.
RUMBLE RUMBLE

BLARRRG
WHAT'S THAT?!

SNAP!

BLOOOOooo

PERFECT.

WHAT. KIND OF ANIMAL IS THAT SUP-POSED TO BE?
I DON'T KNOW. I'M TOO TERRIFIED TO THINK RIGHT NOW.
I WAS JUST THINKING ABOUT HOW I NEEDED THE STICK TO BE EXACTLY THIS HEIGHT.

LET'S GET OUT OF HERE! THAT ROCK THING WAS ENOUGH TO SATISFY MY WEIRD ANIMAL QUOTIENT FOR THE REST OF MY LIFE!

GIDDYUP! YEEHAH!
STAY AWAY FROM THE BIG ROCKS JUST IN CASE!
WILL YOU PLEASE GET THAT STINKY SNAKE CARCASS OFF MY FACE! I CAN'T RUN WHILE WEARING A REPTILE BLINDFOLD!
ALL OF A SUDDEN THIS WHOLE ISLAND FEELS KINDA CREEPY.

REESE, I TOLD YOU TO STAY AWAY FROM THOSE ROCKS! WE DON'T KNOW WHICH ONES ARE NORMAL AND WHICH ONES ARE DANGEROUS!
WELL, IF I FIND THE DANGEROUS KIND AGAIN, IT WILL BE A GOOD CHANCE FOR ME TO PRACTICE MY KARATE MOVES ON IT!
I DIDN'T THINK IT WAS POSSIBLE TO MAKE ME EVEN MORE WORRIED! THANKS, REESE.
NO PROBLEM, MOM. IT'S A GIFT.

WILL YOU QUIT SCREWING AROUND?!
HI-YAH! WHAP-WHAP-POW!

WHOOPS!
SLIP

PLOP

OOF!

DAAAD!

SON! ARE YOU OKAY?!

YEAH, I'M FINE. OTHER THAN I ALMOST JUST KISSED A DEAD GUY.
I'M COMING DOWN!

THIS GUY'S BEEN HIDDEN DOWN HERE A LOOONG TIME.

WHAT ARE YOU BOYS DOING DOWN THERE?
HOLD ON, HONEY! WE'RE FINE.

REESE, I NEED YOU TO GO UP TOP AND KEEP JANIE FROM LOOKING DOWN HERE AND ACCI-DENTALLY SEEING A DEAD GUY! I'LL GO THROUGH HIS STUFF AND BE UP IN A MINUTE.
OKAY, DAD.

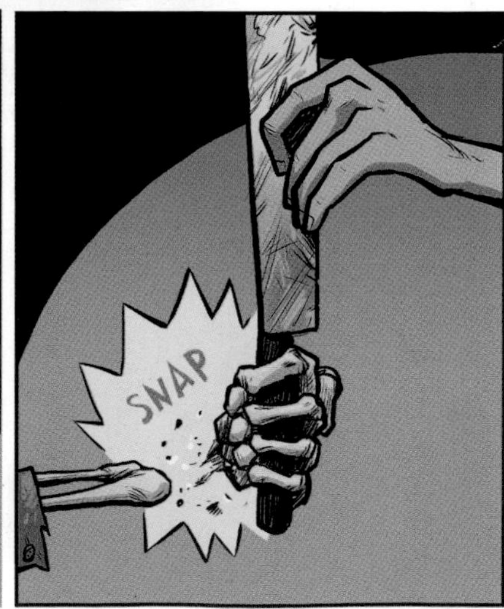
SNAP

AHA!

LYLE, I REALLY THINK WE SHOULD GET BACK TO CAMP. WHAT IF THAT ROCK THING COMES BACK?

I'LL BE RIGHT UP!

CLUNK

WHEW!

HOW LONG HAS THAT YUCKY SKELETON BEEN DOWN THERE?
JANIE! YOU'RE NOT SUPPOSED TO KNOW ABOUT HIM!
I DON'T KNOW HOW LONG HE'S BEEN DOWN THERE...

...BUT WE JUST SCORED HIS JOURNAL! SO WE MIGHT GET SOME ANSWERS ABOUT THIS PLACE!
CAN WE PLEASE JUST GET OUT OF HERE?

SURE. LOOK, IF WE CUT STRAIGHT THROUGH THIS WOOD INSTEAD OF FOLLOWING THE COAST, I THINK WE CAN MAKE IT BACK IN HALF THE TIME!

NEWARK PUBLIC LIBRARY
121 HIGH ST.
NEWARK, NY 14513

ZZZT
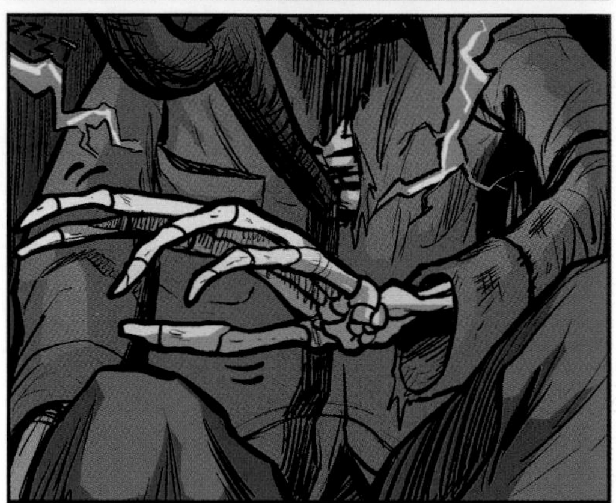

VARKRUSSS.

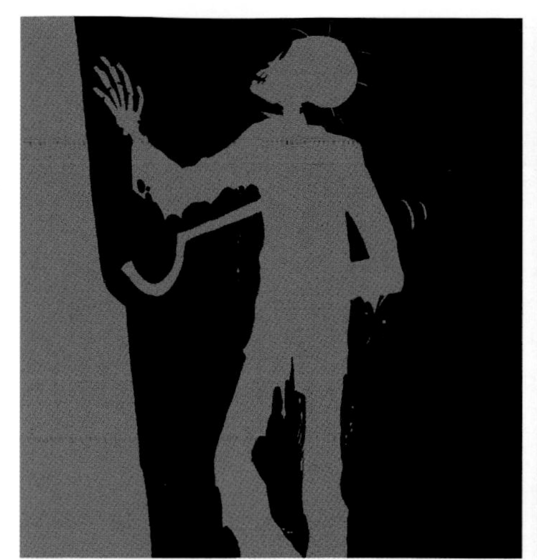

VARKRUSSs...

BUT LOOKIE AT HOW CLOSE THOSE TWO ARE! THEY MUST BE IN LOVE!

CHOMP

GULP

AAEEEK!
JANIE, NO! DON'T SCREA--

REEK
REEK

REEK
REEK
REEK

REEK
REEK
REEK

UH-OH! OUR VISITOR RETURNED!

THIS ISLAND MUST BE INFESTED WITH ALL KINDS OF GROSS ANIMALS! ...I'LL BET THEY FRENCHED OUR STUFF WHILE WE WERE OUT!
IT'S NOT ANIMALS. THEY LEFT OUR FOOD ALONE.
THEY KNOW A LOT ABOUT US AND WE DON'T KNOW ANYTHING ABOUT THEM!

WE NEED ANSWERS.

CRACK

REEK!
REEK!
REEK!

REEK

♪ IT'S RAINING! IT'S POURING! THE OLD MAN IS SNORING! ♫

WHEEEE!

LET'S GET EVERYTHING UNDER THE TARP.

MAN, IT'S REALLY COMING DOWN!
THE JOURNAL!
DAD, I DON'T LIKE THE RAIN ANYMORE!

THIS SHOULD KEEP OUR MINDS OFF OF THE RAIN!

YOU GET TO READ IT!
GOOD! I HOPE THERE'S LOTS OF JUICY PERSONAL INFORMATION THAT'S NONE OF MY BUSINESS!

YOU GET HIS POCKETKNIFE! DON'T CUT OFF YOUR FINGERS.
COOL!

AND I GET TO FIGURE OUT THIS...THING. WHATEVER IT IS.
DON'T I GET ANY-THING?

SURE! YOU GET THIS PURSE!

I'LL BET PICKLES WOULD PREFER TO STAY IN HERE WHERE PEOPLE CAN'T SMELL HIM--UH, I MEAN, SO HE CAN GET SOME REST!
OH, THAT WILL BE JUST PERFECT!

GOOD NIGHT IN THERE!

IT SAYS HERE THAT HIS NAME WAS G. K. HIGGENBOTHAM. THERE'RE ONLY THREE ENTRIES, WITH THE LAST ONE DATED JUNE 13, 1891!

DOES IT SAY HOW HE GOT HERE?
HE STOWED AWAY ON A SHIPPING BARGE AND CAME HERE LOOKING FOR SOMETHING.

HE FOUND AN ARTIFACT. LOOK FAMILIAR?
artifact

HUH. AN ARTIFACT.

I DON'T LIKE HIS LAST ENTRY...

..."SOME-THING IS TRACKING ME."

WHOA.

THAT'S OUR ISLAND!

SNAP

HAVE YOU BEEN STUDYING THAT THING ALL NIGHT?
I THINK I'VE GOT IT FIGURED OUT. COME AND SEE THIS!

IT'S MOVING!
LOOK! EVERY TIME I TOUCH THE CORNERS OF THE TILE, IT CHANGES THE IMAGE.

HERE'S A BUNCH OF PLANTS.
THOSE ARE ALL SPECIES I'VE SEEN SINCE WE GOT HERE!

LOOK AT THIS LIST OF ANIMALS, KAREN! THERE'S THE ROCK CREATURE WE SAW ON OUR HIKE YESTERDAY.
WE'VE SEEN THESE FUNNY LITTLE BIRD THINGS, TOO.

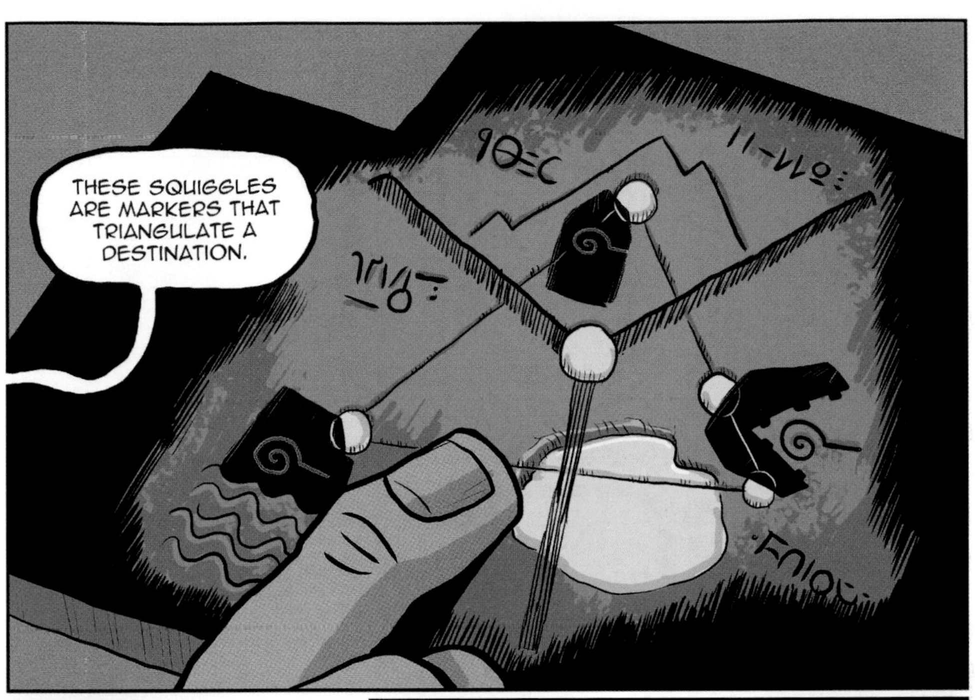
THESE SQUIGGLES ARE MARKERS THAT TRIANGULATE A DESTINATION.

I'VE SEEN THAT SHAPE BEFORE!

JANIE, DO THESE SQUIGGLES LOOK FAMILIAR?

THE "HIDING PLACE"!

WHAT ARE YOU KIDS TALKING ABOUT?

WE SAW THIS SYMBOL ON A ROCK ON OUR WAY OUT TO THE RIVER!

JANIE THOUGHT SHE HEARD SOMEONE SAY "HIDING PLACE."

THIS IS SOME KIND OF MAP.
TO WHERE?

THAT'S YOUR JOB TO FIGURE OUT!
BUT I CAN'T READ THIS GOBBLEDYGOOK!

I BELIEVE IN YOU.

YOU CAN'T FOOL ME WITH YOUR MOTIVATIONAL-SPEAKER TALK! YOU'RE UP TO SOMETHING, RIGHT? WHAT HAVE YOU GOT PLANNED, LYLE?
YOU'LL SEE.
IS THIS ENOUGH?
THAT'S PERFECT! JUST THROW THEM OVER HERE!

UH!
PLOP

DAD, WHAT ARE WE SUPPOSED TO BE MAKING?
YOU'LL SEE.

ISSSSS...
HAH!!
PING
CHOOM

FLING
AWKS?

BLAAARRR
WE GOT IT! REESE, HELP ME TIE IT UP!

WHAT DID
WE CATCH?

I DON'T KNOW!
I'VE NEVER SEEN
ANYTHING LIKE IT!

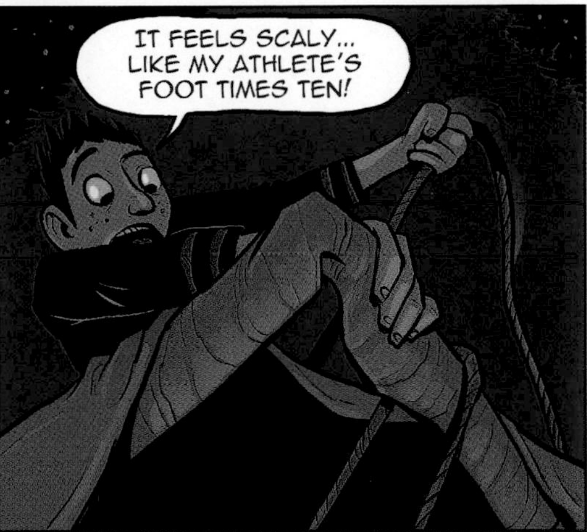
IT FEELS SCALY...
LIKE MY ATHLETE'S
FOOT TIMES TEN!

GAH!

THAT TREE...
IT'S MOVING!
ZZZT

CREEEAK
GET OUTTA MY
PANTS, CREEP!

HROOOAAR

LET THIS THING GO BEFORE HE MAKES THAT TREE EAT ALL OF US!

THUD
HERE, KAREN! TAKE THIS!

SPUT
AAAAAH! IT WANTS THE ARTIFACT!
ZZZ.
SWACK
CHONK
HROOOARR
CUTTING THE VINES ONLY MAKES IT ANGRIER!

HREEEEE

GLARG

GO ON! GET OUT OF HERE OR MY DAD WILL ATTACK YOU WITH HIS FRYING PAN AGAIN!
BLAAAAAAAA

AW, THE VISITOR GOT AWAY.
BUT AT LEAST HE DIDN'T GET THIS!

SOONER OR LATER HE'S GOING TO TAKE IT FROM US.

SNORE

SHE'S GOT THE RIGHT IDEA. WE SHOULD ALL TRY TO GET SOME SLEEP.

FIRST THING TOMORROW WE'LL FOLLOW THE MAP AND FIND OUT WHAT OUR VISITOR DOESN'T WANT US TO KNOW.
USE IT OR LOSE IT.

I'LL STAND GUARD.

...WITH MY FRYING PAN.

I'M GONNA SLEEP OUT HERE, JUST IN CASE YOU NEED MY HELP.
DAD?
YEAH?
DON'T YOU THINK WE'RE IN OVER OUR HEADS OUT HERE?
PROBABLY.
SO, I DON'T GET WHY YOU'RE NOT SCARED.

I DON'T BELIEVE I EVER TOLD YOU THE STORY ABOUT WHAT HAPPENED THE DAY AFTER YOU WERE BORN...

...YOU HAD JUST FINISHED NURSING, SO MOM HANDED YOU TO ME FOR BURPING...

...I PATTED YOU ON THE BACK AND YOU DIDN'T RESPOND. MIND YOU, THIS IS ONLY THE THIRD TIME I'D EVER HELD A BABY...

UH-OH, HE'S GOT MILK GUNK IN HIS MOUTH.
IS HE BREATHING?

KAREN! HE'S NOT BREATHING! WHAT AM I SUPPOSED TO DO NOW?!

I DON'T KNOW! TRY PATTING HIM ON THE BACK!

PAT
PAT
PAT
IT'S NOT WORKING! HIS FACE IS TURNING BLUE!

I'LL BUZZ FOR THE NURSE!
HELP! CAN SOMEONE HELP US?!

HELP! OUR BABY'S CHOKING!
2A

I'VE GOT HIM. I'LL SHOW YOU WHAT TO DO IN CASE THIS EVER HAPPENS AGAIN.

TURN HIM ON HIS SIDE AND SQUEEZE THE ASPIRATOR...

...PUT IT IN THE BACK OF THE THROAT AND LET IT SUCK OUT THE MUCUS. SEE?
SLURP

PULL IT OUT TO SEE IF THE BREATHING PASSAGE IS CLEARED... AND LOOK! HE'S BREATHING AGAIN.
GASP

OKAY?

NIRVANA

ARE YOU GOING TO BE OKAY?

I DON'T KNOW. I DON'T KNOW ANYTHING RIGHT NOW.
ON THAT DAY, I WAS SCARED AS HELL...

...BUT SINCE THAT DAY, AS LONG AS MY FAMILY IS OKAY, NOTHING CAN EVER FREAK ME OUT.

IF YOU'RE OKAY, THEN NOTHING CAN EVER SCARE ME.

I...I HAD PACKED A BAG BEFORE WE LEFT, BECAUSE I WAS GOING TO RUN AWAY.

I KNEW THAT, SON. THAT'S WHY I DECIDED TO TAKE THE WHOLE FAMILY ON A LITTLE BOAT TRIP.

BOM
BOM
BOM
DESTROY!!!
BREAK THEM!

WE MUST PROTECT THE CIVILIZATIONS ON OUR BACKS! IF YOU LOVE ME, MATE, YOU WILL LET ME GO TO BATTLE!
BUT SURELY A KINGDOM CANNOT RISK LOSING ITS KING! PLEASE, DON'T GO!

THE HEARTS OF THE PEOPLE WILL BE STRENGTHENED WHEN THEY SEE THEIR KING IN BATTLE!
BESIDES, IF I FAIL, THE KINGDOM WILL LIVE ON THROUGH OUR SON.

DAD, I'M READY TO JOIN YOU IN BATTLE, BUT MY SUBJECTS HAVE ABANDONED THEIR POSTS! THEY WON'T PUT ME IN BATTLE MODE!
SEE WHAT YOU HAVE DONE? NOW EVEN YOUR SON HAS A LUST FOR WAR!
MY SON...

...MY ONE AND ONLY SON. THERE WILL ALWAYS BE WARS TO FIGHT. WHEN YOU ARE A LITTLE OLDER, WE WILL FIGHT SIDE BY SIDE, I PROMISE.
BUT I AM ALREADY 6,542 YEARS OLD! MY WHISKERS ARE ALREADY COMING IN!
I WARN YOU, DO NOT DEFY ME.

...I HAVE NOTHING MORE TO SAY ABOUT IT!

I KNOW YOU ARE SAD, SON. BUT YOU MUST BE PROTECTED NO MATTER WHAT! THE THRONE MUST SURVIVE THIS ATTACK OR THE KINGDOM WILL BE LOST!
LEAVE ME ALONE!

I AM FINISHED BEING TREATED LIKE A BABY!

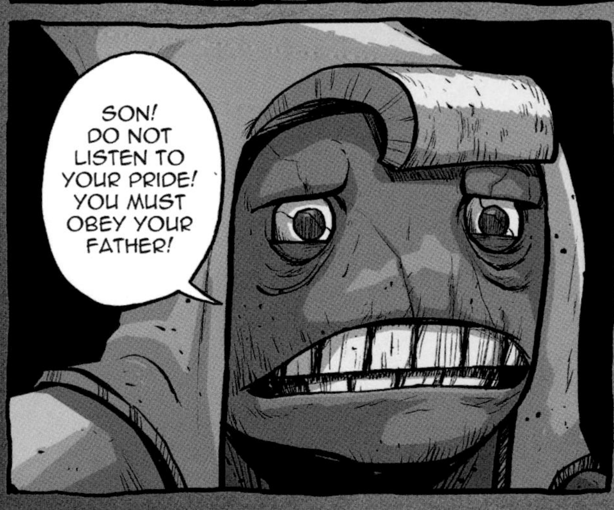
SON! DO NOT LISTEN TO YOUR PRIDE! YOU MUST OBEY YOUR FATHER!

GOOD-BYE, MOTHER!

FIRST I NEED TO CONSUME ENERGY!

FATHER'S PRIVATE STOCK IS A MEAL FIT FOR A WARRIOR!
CHOMP
CHOMP
CHOMP

PRINCE, YOU KNOW YOU ARE NOT ALLOWED TO EAT FROM THAT PEN!
HA! I AM GOING TO WAR! IT COULD BE DAYS BEFORE I GET TO EAT AGAIN!

IN FACT, I COULD USE YOUR HELP! I NEED YOU TO PLUG IN MY BATTLE PROGRAM... ...AND DO NOT WORRY. I WILL NOT TELL MY FATHER!
BUT WE CANNOT DISOBEY AN ORDER OF THE KING!

I AM GOING INTO BATTLE WITH OR WITHOUT YOUR HELP. IF YOU DO NOT ACTIVATE MY ARMOR, I WILL GO REGARDLESS!
I AM SORRY, PRINCE.

SO BE IT!

HROARRRR
YOU WERE WRONG ABOUT ME, FATHER!
BIM
BIM
BIM
I AM OLD ENOUGH TO BE A WARRIOR!

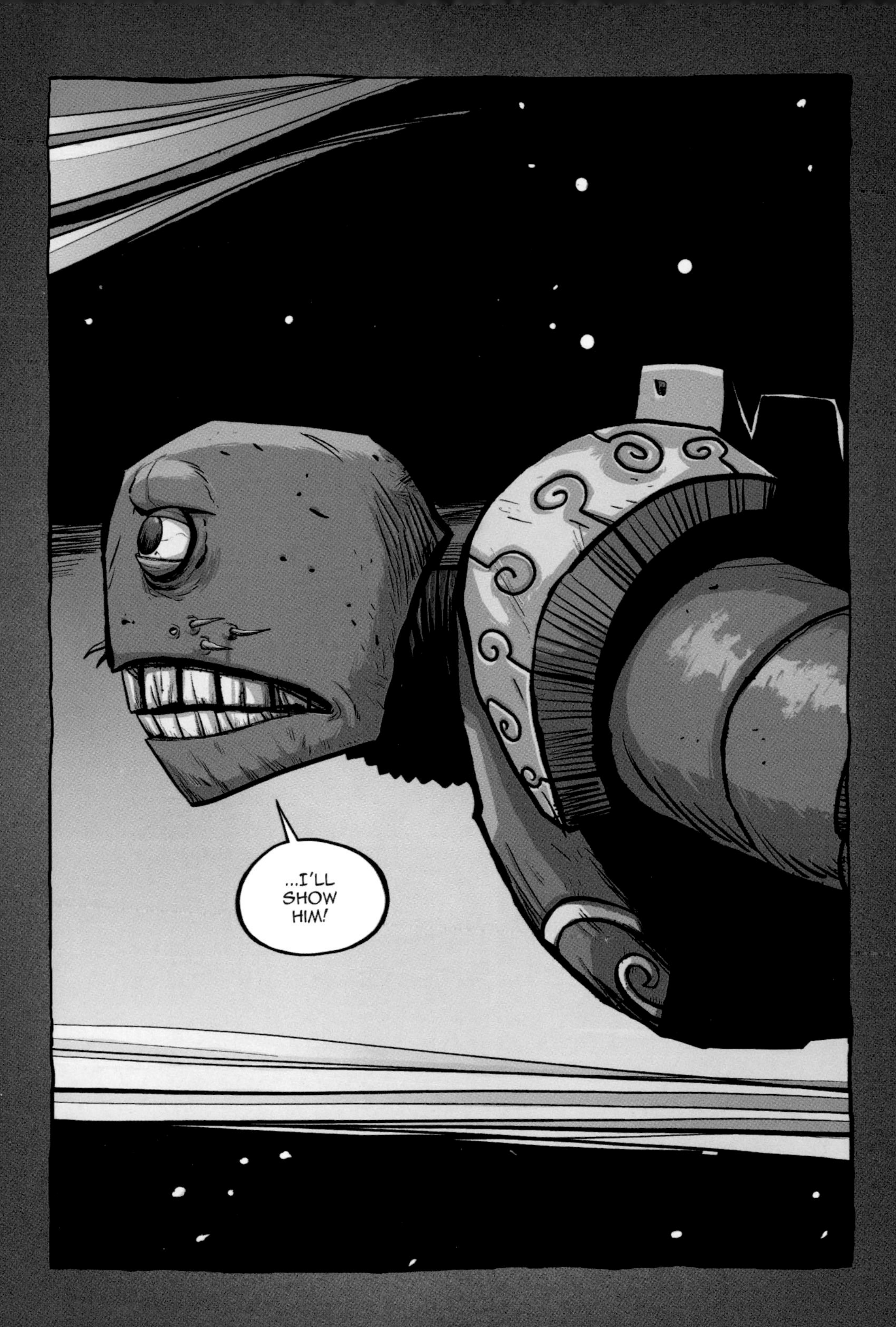
...I'LL SHOW HIM!

CHOMP
SLURP
GULP
SLURP
HURRY UP, HONEY!

SLUUURP

I AM, SHEESH!
WATCH YOUR TONE, YOUNG LADY!
OKAY, REESE. THINK YOU CAN FIND THAT ROCK WITH THE SQUIGGLE ON IT AGAIN?

I DON'T KNOW IF I CAN FIND IT...

...WITHOUT JANIE'S HELP!

I'LL TAKE THE LEAD!

IF WE RUN INTO TROUBLE, STICK TOGETHER! IF WE GET SEPA-RATED, MAKE YOUR WAY BACK TO CAMP AS FAST AS YOU CAN.

OH, I'LL BE READY FOR TROUBLE, ALL RIGHT!

IT'S UP HERE, EVERYBODY! IT'S RIGHT HERE!

THAT'S IT, ALL RIGHT!
I KNEW WE COULD FIND IT!

OUR DESTINATION IS SOUTH OF THIS ROCK!

SO, WE GOOOOO...

...JUST THROUGH THOSE TREES.
THAT'S SOME DENSE FOLIAGE.

SHINGG
IT'S NO MATCH FOR MY BLADE!

HACK

LYLE, I'M IMPRESSED! WHERE DID YOU LEARN TO USE A MACHETE LIKE THAT?
IT'S A MAN THING.

HACK
CHOP

CHONK
HAH!

SLASH

UH!
THUNK
WHEW.
HUH!
CHOP
THWACK

YOU DID GREAT, SWEETIE!

MY TURN! MY TURN!

SMOOCH!

COME ON, DADDY!
PLEH

WHACK

THIS IS THE DEAD CENTER OF THAT ARTIFACT MAP.
I'VE NEVER SEEN THIS STYLE OF ARCHITEC-TURE BEFORE.

SOMETHING IS INSIDE!

WE'VE SEEN THIS GUY BEFORE. IT'S MR. CARNIVOROUS TREE!

MAYBE HE CAME OUT OF THAT CAN!

BUT WHERE DID ALL OF THESE COME FROM?

THERE IS A CANISTER FOR EVERY PLANT ON THE ISLAND!

HMMM...
MEEP

BWAAA
WHAT DID YOU DO?! DID YOU TOUCH SOME-THING?
I ONLY TOUCHED AN IMAGE OF A CRITTER!

BWAAA

VOOMP

MOCK MOCK

AW, LOOK! IT'S JUST A LITTLE BABY! CAN I KEEP IT?
PLOP

IS THERE A BUTTON ON THE ARTIFACT THAT LOOKS LIKE A CHOCOLATE CAKE?

NOPE. THIS ISLAND WAS POPU-LATED ONLY BY HOSTILE CREATURES... ...AND I THINK IT WAS INTENTIONAL!
BUT WHO WOULD DO THAT? THE MILITARY? SOME GREEDY, CORRUPT CORPORA-TION?

SON, YOU'VE WATCHED TOO MANY MOVIES.
THEN WHO? ...CANADA?

THAT THING THAT VISITED OUR CAMP SURE WAS INTERESTED IN GETTING THE ARTIFACT! MAYBE HE DID IT.
WAIT. WHERE'S JANIE?
DAD.
HELLO, LITTLE, TINY MAN!

MY NAME IS JANIE! WHAT'S YOUR NAME?

JANIE, STOP!

AIIEEEEE
MO-MO!

DAD-DEEEE!
MO-MO
MOMO-MO
CH-CHONK
UH!
MO!
CHONK
SLASH
MO!
MO MO
MO-MO
MO
MO-MO

MO!
MO
MO

HANDOFF!

REESE! GET YOUR SISTER BACK TO CAMP!

KLONG

GO, REESE! GO!
MO-MOMO
MO-MO!
MO-MO

HOLD ON TIGHT, SIS! WE'RE GONNA BREAK THAT LINE!
MO!
MO-MO!
MO-MO-MO!

HIT!

LIFT!

DRIVE!

THAT'S MY BOY!

MO-MO
MO-MO!
MO
MO-MO!

MO-MO
MO-MO!

MO-
MO-MO-
MO-
PICKLES!

POW

FOOM
MO-MO!
MO-MO!

RRRRKK!

Mo-Mo!
Mo-Mo-Mo
Mo!

Mo-Mo!
Mo-
Mo!
Mo-
Mo-
Mo!

Mo-
Mo-
Mo!
MO!
Mo-
Mo!
Mo-
Mo

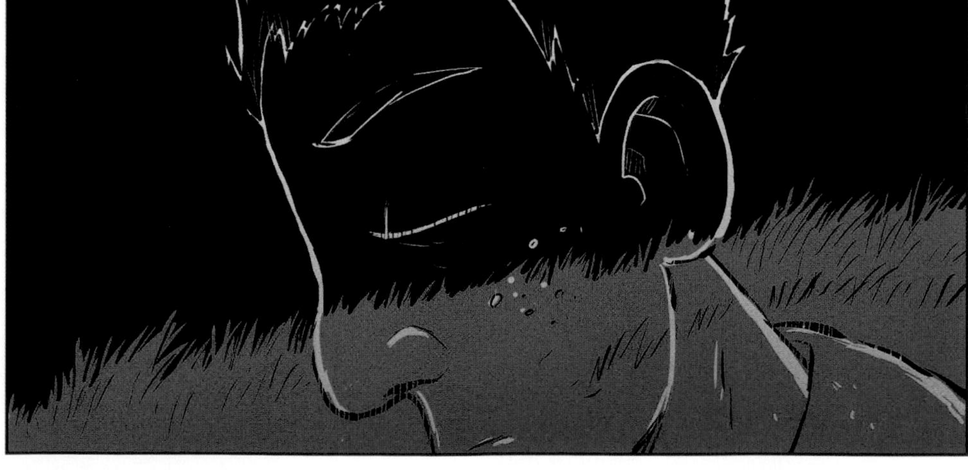

HIDING PLACE

WHO WAS THAT GIANT THING?
I DON'T KNOW. BUT I THINK HE'S A GOOD GUY.

DAD SAID THAT IF WE GET SEPARATED WE'RE SUPPOSED TO GO BACK TO CAMP!
WE'RE NOT GOING BACK TO CAMP.

BUT DAD SAID--
NEVER MIND THAT.

WE'VE GOTTA GET MOM AND DAD BACK!

KAREN, I WANT YOU TO KNOW HOW SORRY I AM THAT I TOOK THE FAMILY ON THIS TRIP!
AND I WANT TO LET YOU KNOW HOW SORRY I AM THAT WE CAME ALONG.

...BUT I STILL LOVE YOU MORE THAN ANYTHING!

UH!

MO.
MO.

ARE YOU OKAY?
I'M GOOD...

...IT'S THE KIDS THAT I'M WORRIED ABOUT.

OKAY, JANIE. IT'S SAFE FOR US TO MOVE OUT!
WE ARE RIGHT BEHIND YOU!

SQUEAK
"WE"?

EXCUSE ME, BUT JUST WHAT IS THAT THING?

I FOUND HIM ON THE TRAIL. HE'S MY NEW PET!
YOU PUT THAT THING DOWN RIGHT NOW! WE DON'T HAVE TIME FOR THIS!

BUT HE RAN AWAY FROM HIS MOMMA AND CAN'T FIND HIS WAY HOME!

WAAAAH

SHHH! DO YOU WANT EVERY FREAK MONSTER WITHIN EARSHOT TO HEAR US?!

I'LL TELL YOU WHAT. AS LONG AS YOU KEEP QUIET, YOU CAN KEEP HIM. DEAL?
DEAL.

OH, REESE! YOU ARE THE BESTEST BROTHER EVER!

SQU-EAK

...AND YOU'D BETTER STOP YOUR SQUEAKIN' OR I'LL GIVE YOU THE BOOT!

ARE YOU AWAKE, LYLE?
MOSTLY.

DO YOU THINK THAT REESE AND JANIE MADE IT BACK TO CAMP?
NOPE.

WHAT DO YOU MEAN?! YOU DON'T THINK THAT THEY'RE OKAY?

THEY'RE OKAY, BUT THEY DIDN'T GO BACK TO CAMP. WHEN WAS THE LAST TIME REESE DID WHAT I ASKED HIM TO DO?

THEN WHERE DID THEY GO?
REESE DOESN'T THINK I NOTICED, BUT BEFORE WE LEFT HE TOOK THE FLARE GUN! IF THEY'RE NOT IN HERE, THEN THEY'RE JUST FINE!

MO!

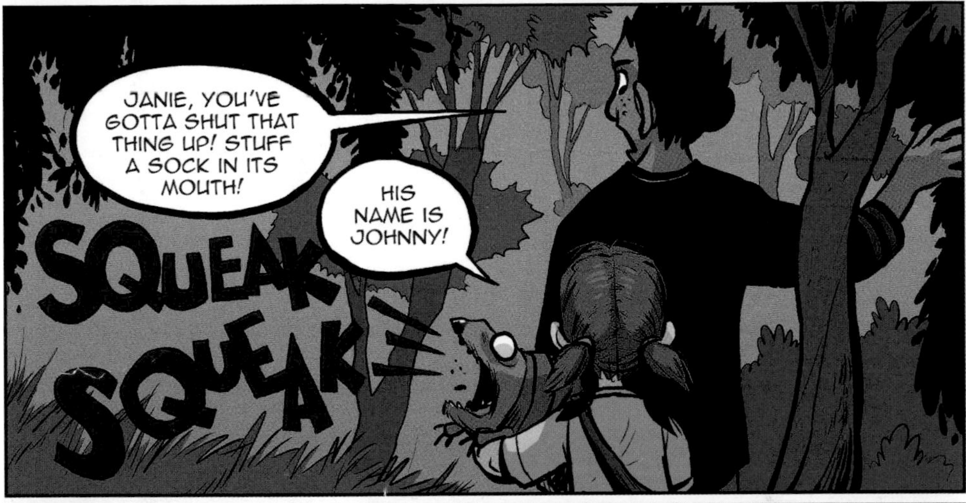
JANIE, YOU'VE GOTTA SHUT THAT THING UP! STUFF A SOCK IN ITS MOUTH!
HIS NAME IS JOHNNY!
SQUEAK
SQUEAK

AH-AH AH-AH

PIFF
TONK
ACHOO

HE COULD'VE KILLED US!

BYE-BYE, JOHNNY!

BOOT
NO!

NOW QUIT MESSING AROUND AND LET'S GO!

FORGET IT! NOTHING YOU SAY IS GONNA MAKE ME MOVE NOW!

HURLL

OH, CRUD.

HURLLL

CHOMK

NICE AND EASY... ...JUST DON'T LOOK DOWN!

HURRL
HURRY, REESE! IT'S RIGHT BEHIND YOU!

CRACK

HUURRR

FOOM

OH, MAN.

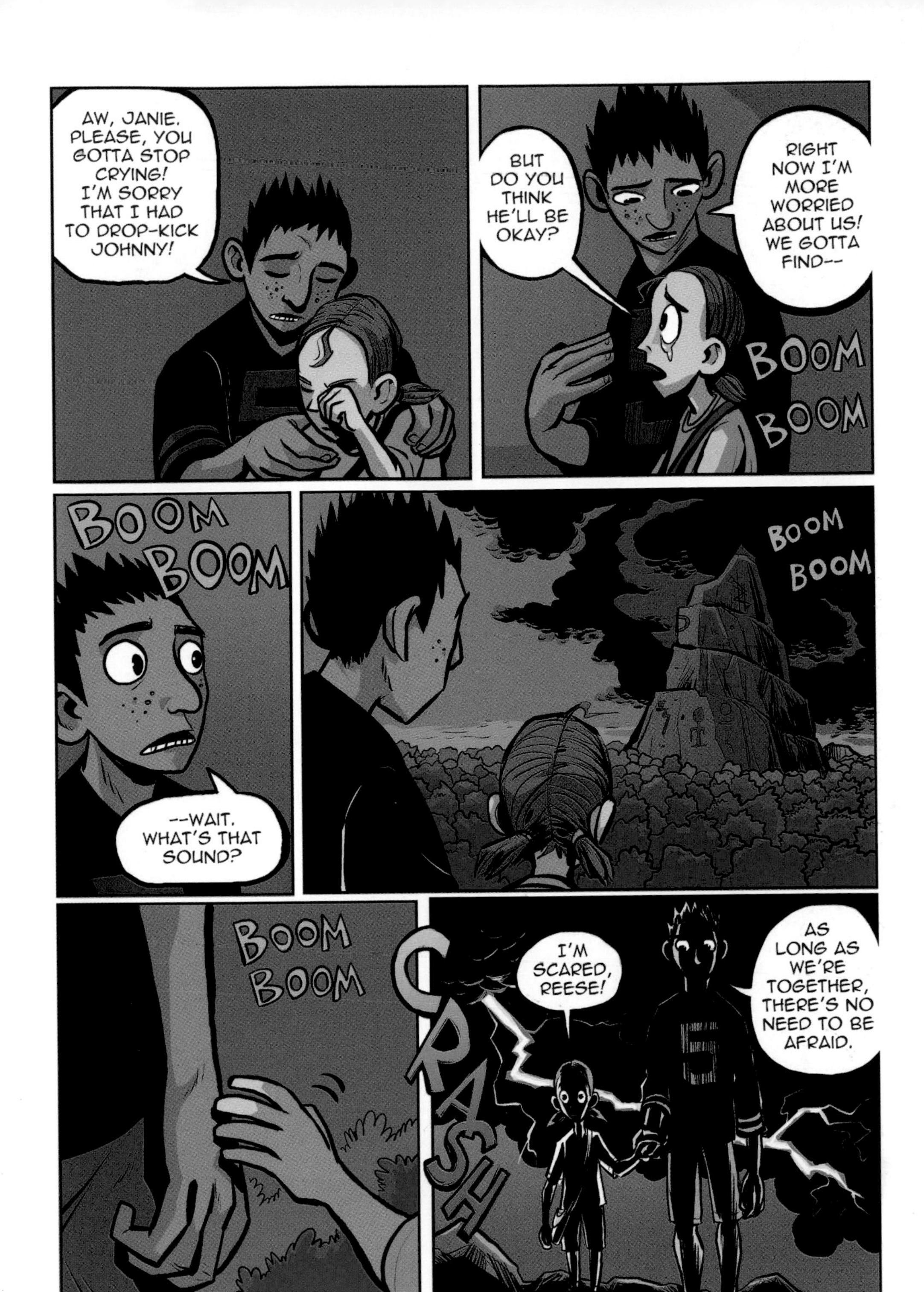

NEWARK PUBLIC LIBRARY
121 HIGH ST.
NEWARK, NY 14513

THIS GREEN GUNK IS BURNING MY NOSE!
MO-MO-MO
BY THE SMELL I'D SAY IT'S HYDROCHLORIC ACID.
MO-MO
MO-MO
BOOM BOOM
BOOM BOOM
BOOM BOOM
BOOM BOOM

BOOM BOOM
MO-MO
MO!
MO.
HEY, WATCH WHERE YOU POINT THAT STICK, BUB!
BLOOP

UH. ARGH!
LYLE, THIS IS THE SAME KIND OF ACID OUR STOMACHS USE FOR DIGESTION!
BOOM BOOM

BOOM BOOM
WHAT ARE YOU WORKING ON BACK THERE?
I'M USING OUR HOUSE KEYS TO SAW MY HANDS FREE. BUT I NEED MORE TIME!

COME ON, KAREN. THINK OF SOMETHING YOU CAN DO TO INTERRUPT THEIR CEREMONY!
BOOM
BOOM

MOMOMO MO! MO-MO MO!
HEY, YOU GUYS!

UH, I NEED TO USE THE LITTLE LADIES' ROOM. DO YOU KNOW WHAT THAT IS?

MOMOMOMO!

I DON'T THINK THEY HAVE A LADIES' ROOM.
NO! THEY STOPPED THE DRUMS FOR A BIT! KEEP BUG-GING THEM!

BOOM BOOM
YOU GOTTA COME UP WTH SOMETHING QUICK! WE DON'T WANT TO GET TO THE END OF THE RITUAL!

OH, SAY CAN YOU SEE--

MO?
--BY THE DAWN'S EARLY LIGHT--

--WHAT SO PROUDLY WE HAILED--

-AT THE TWILIGHT'S LAST GLEAMING?
I'M ALMOST THROUGH IT!

I THINK I SPRAINED A LUNG.
GIVE ME JUST A FEW MORE-- WHOOPS!

PLOP

WHAT WAS THAT PLOP? DON'T TELL ME THAT WAS WHAT I THINK IT WAS!

MOMO-MOMO!

NO, WAIT!

KONK

PLOP

WHO THREW THAT ROCK?

MOMO!

I'VE GOT A LOT MORE WHERE THAT CAME FROM!

IT'S THE KIDS!

BASH

MO-
MO
MO!

THIS WAY, JANIE!

MO-
MO!
MO!

MOMO-MO!
MO-MO!
MO!
MO-
MO
O!

CLANG
SNAP

WHOA!

THUNK

HOY!

GLOSH

STAY CLOSE TO ME, JANIE! I'LL THINK OF SOME-THING!
MO-MO-MO!
MO!

MO-MO!
OH, COME ON, GUYS! WAIT--WAIT--LET'S TALK!

YOU WANT ME TO COME WITH YOU?

BOP
HERE!

SPUT

GAH!
FSSSSS

GUSH

GREAT, NOW I'M STUCK ON AN ISLAND ON AN ISLAND!

HE'S BURNING OUT FROM UNDER ME!

I'M COMING, DAD!

PUUUSH!

HAVE A NICE TRIP!

FSSSSSS

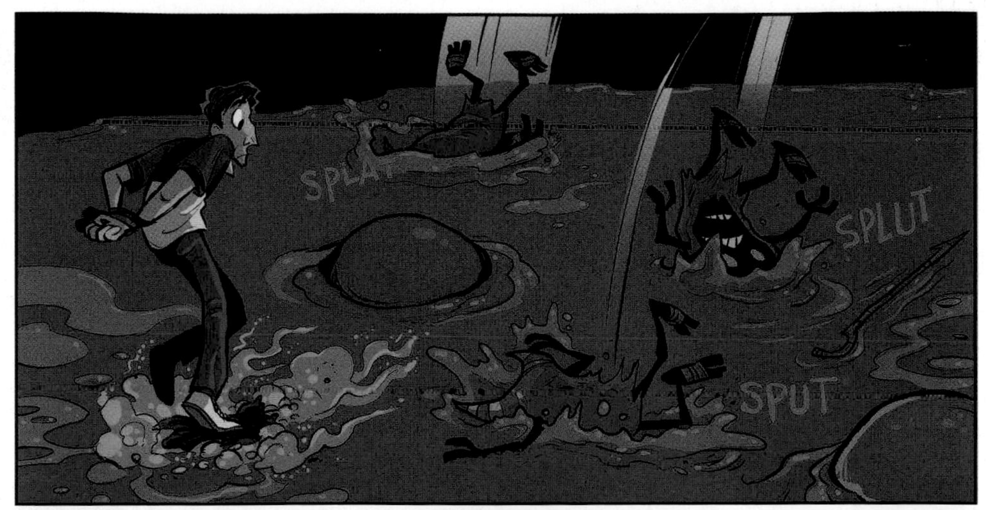
SPLAT
SPLUT
SPUT

THAT'LL WORK!

THANKS, HONEY!
NO PROB.
PING

WOW! THIS IS A REALLY BAD ISLA--

TONK

GOTTA KEEP MOVING!

JANIE, MY GIRL!
DADDY! MOMMY!

I DON'T SEE A WAY OUT OF THIS ONE! WHAT DO WE DO NOW?

SQUEAK!
OMO?
OMO?
OMO-OMO?

SQUEAK!

JOHNNY, YOU FOUND US!
WHO IS JOHNNY?

MO!
MO-MO
MO-MO
MO!
MO-MO
MO!
MO-MO!
MO-MO-MO!

GRAARRR

WHOMP

CHOMP

GULP

BASH
SPUT

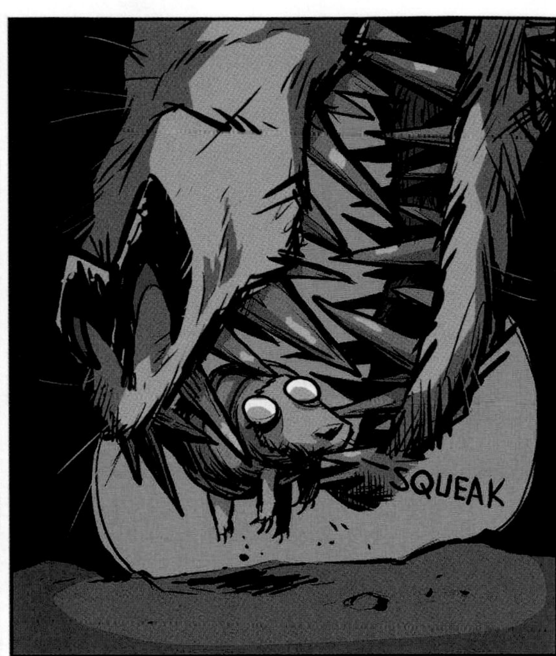
SQUEAK

PLOP

SQUEAK!
SQUEAK!
SQUEAK!

MOOOOOOOO

THUNK
RAAAAA

SNIFF
SNIFF

SHE'S GONNA SNEEZE!

AH-AH
AH-AH
QUICK! GET BEHIND THIS ROCK!

THOO
THOO
THOO
THUNK
TONK
THOO
THOO
ACHOO

ZIP
WHIFF
WHUP
THONK

WHUP
THUNK
ZIP

GROOOARR

SQUEAK
SQUEAK
SQUEAK

GRRRRRR

I DON'T SPEAK BABY MONSTER, BUT I THINK HE JUST TOLD HIS MOMMA THAT I DROP-KICKED HIM!

EVERYONE PLAY DEAD!
THAT'S FOR BEARS, KAREN! THIS THING EATS BEARS!

DAD, LOOK! SOMEONE IS MAKING A DOOR FOR US!
SCRATCH

SQUEAK
SQUEAK
SQUEAK
RAAA

IN HERE!

FASTER!

SLAM

IT'S TOO DARK IN HERE! I DON'T LIKE THE DARK!
WE'RE RIGHT HERE WITH YOU!
DON'T BE AFRAID OF THE DARK... ...ESPECIALLY WHEN ALL OF THE MONSTERS ARE OUTSIDE!

PICKLES IS STARTING TO SMELL KINDA BAD.

LET'S FIND A PLACE TO BURY HIM. HE REEKS!
I DON'T THINK I'M READY TO SAY GOOD-BYE TO HIM YET.

THIS APPEARS TO BE THE ONLY WAY OUT OF THE ROOM.
I'M ALL FOR ANYTHING THAT GETS US OUT OF HERE!

YOU KNOW YOU'RE IN A BAD SITUATION WHEN CRAWLING DEEPER INTO A SPOOKY CAVE BECOMES THE BEST WAY TO GET AWAY FROM MONSTERS!

SNIFF
SNIFF

HISSS

ZZT
ZZT
CHULKOTH!
ROARR

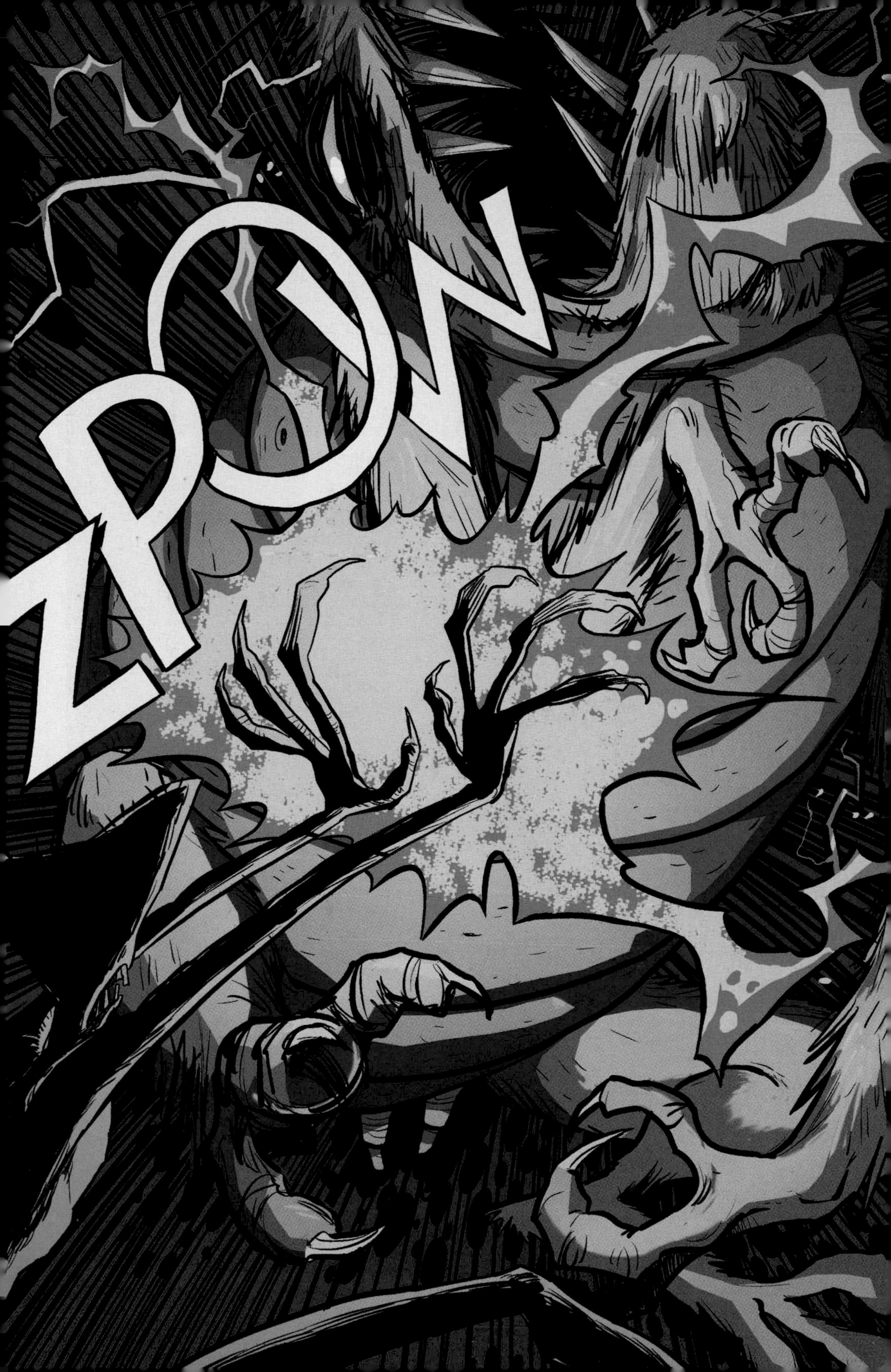
ZPOW

YIPE
YIPE

OKKEKKON!

CREEAK

I SPY, WITH MY LITTLE EYE...
DARKNESS.
YEAH.

IT SMELLS LIKE DEATH IN HERE!
OH, THAT'S JUST JANIE'S STUPID SNAKE!

I HEARD THAT, AND HE'S NOT STUPID!

WHOOOOOOA!

HOLY CROW!

DADDY! I DON'T LIKE THESE MONSTER SKULLS!

THEY'VE BEEN DEAD A LOOONG TIME, JANIE. THEY CAN'T HURT US NOW.
PAT
PAT

KLUNK

CLUMP
CLUMP
SHUFFLE

WHAT'S MAKING THAT NOISE?
HUFF! HUH! HUH!
WHATEVER IT IS, LET'S GO IN THE OPPOSITE DIRECTION!
THAT SOUNDS LIKE A GOOD ENOUGH PLAN TO ME!

MOM, WHAT IF WHATEVER IT IS THAT MADE THESE CREATURES INTO SKELETONS CAN ALSO TURN US INTO SKELETONS?
THIS STREAM OF HYDRO-CHLORIC ACID COULD EASILY BURN THE FLESH OFF OF ALL THESE BONES.

FOLLOW ME THIS WAY! BUT BE CAREFUL WHERE YOU STEP!
WE'RE RIGHT BEHIND YOU, HONEY! YOU'RE DOING GREAT!

CLUNKY
CLUNKETY
CLUNK
I HEAR IT GETTING CLOSER!
WE NEED TO PICK UP THE PACE A LITTLE MORE!
EVERYONE, KEEP YOUR EYES OPEN FOR AN EXIT!
ARGUSSS!
ZZAP
ZAP

ZZZT
ZAP

DAD!
SNAP!

JANIE!
AAAAAAAAA

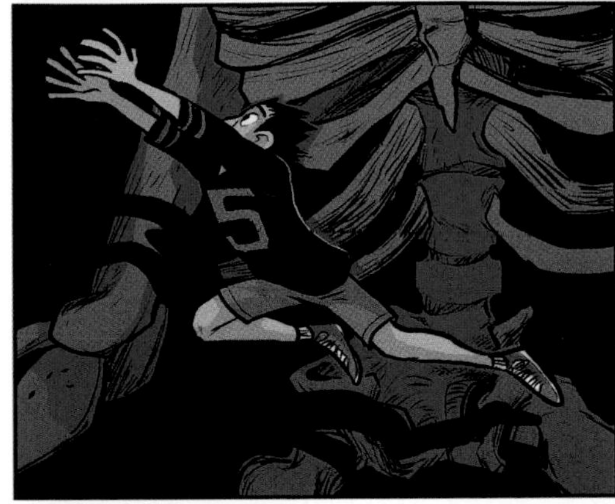

RIP

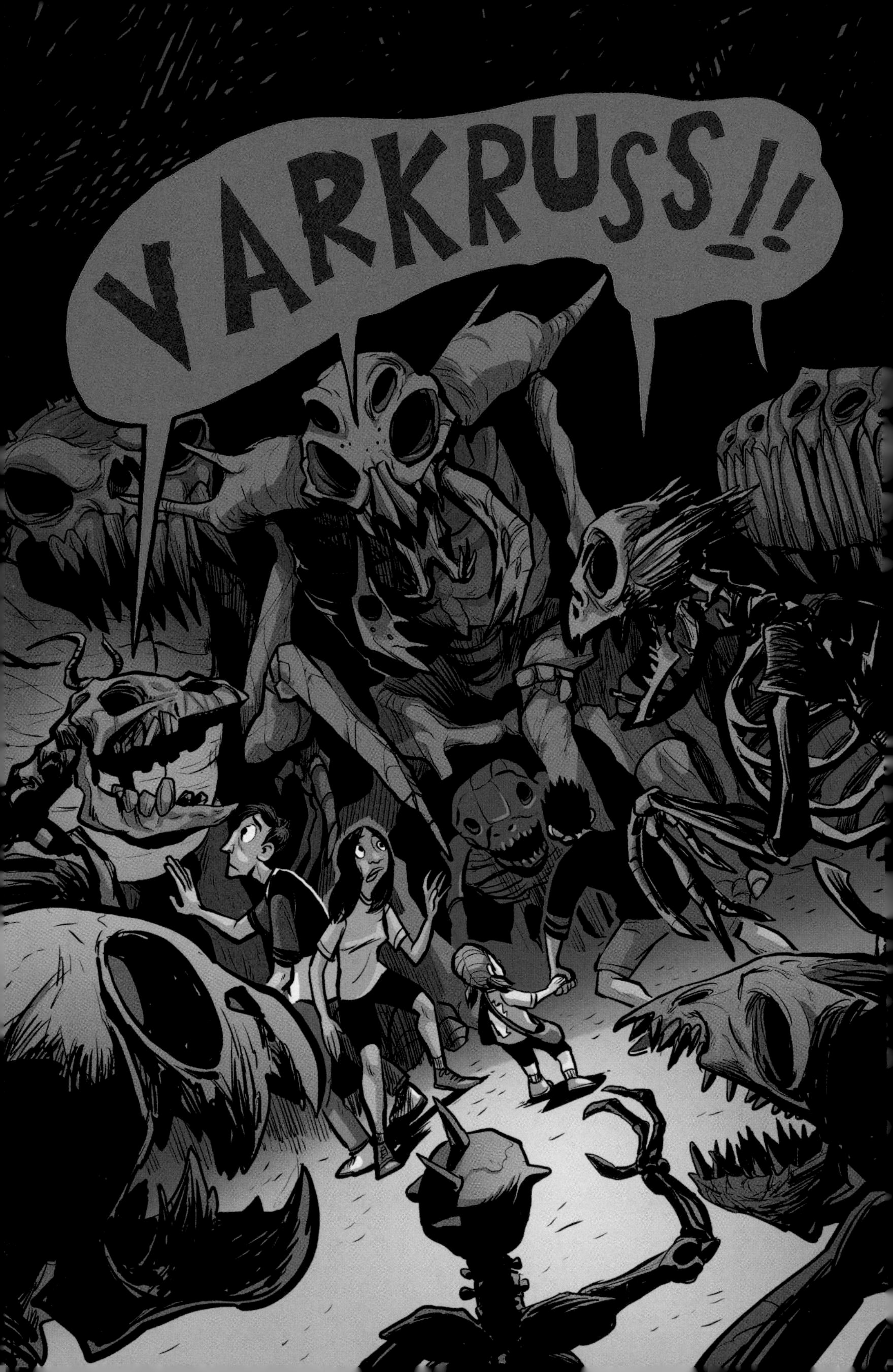
VARKRUSS!!

RUN!

I SEE A LIGHT AHEAD!

GET OUT, BEFORE THEY FULLY ASSEMBLE!
THROUGH HERE!

THEY'RE TRYING TO CUT US OFF!
THEY'RE TOO BIG TO FOLLOW US IN HERE!

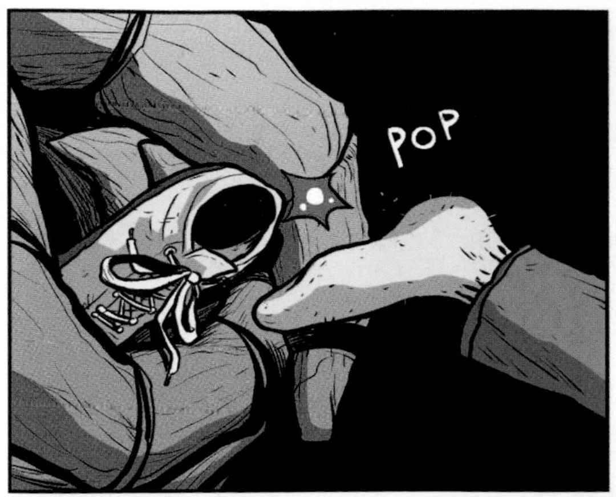
POP

TSSSAAAA!

WE DID IT!
WE'RE IN A GIANT MOUTH!
LET'S CLIMB DOWN THE CHIN AND HEAD BACK TO CAMP!

DAD! A SQUIGGLE JUST APPEARED ON THE ROOF OF THE MOUTH!
FORGET ABOUT THAT! WE'RE GOING THIS WAY!

I DON'T THINK WE'RE SUPPOSED TO GO OUT THE MOUTH! WE SHOULD GO UP TO THAT SQUIGGLE!

NO, REESE. WE'RE NOT GOING UP INTO THAT FISSURE! IF WE DID, WE WOULD BE TRAPPED UP THERE BY THAT THING THAT IS FOLLOWING US! THIS MOUTH APPEARS TO BE THE ONLY EXIT!
I DON'T KNOW WHY, BUT I THINK THIS PLACE IS DRAWING US UP THERE!

NO OFFENSE, BUT I'M NOT GOING TO TRUST YOU OVER MY OWN PLAN!

YOU CAN TRUST ME, DAD.

YOU KNOW WHAT, REESE? YOU'RE RIGHT. YOU'VE DEMONSTRATED YOURSELF TO BE A CAPABLE LEADER!

UP, UP, UP WE GO!

IT'S HERE!

HERAASSS

BASH
UH!

ROARR
I WILL DEFEAT YOU ONE LEG AT A TIME!
NOOOOOOOO!
SNAP

GAH!
CHONK

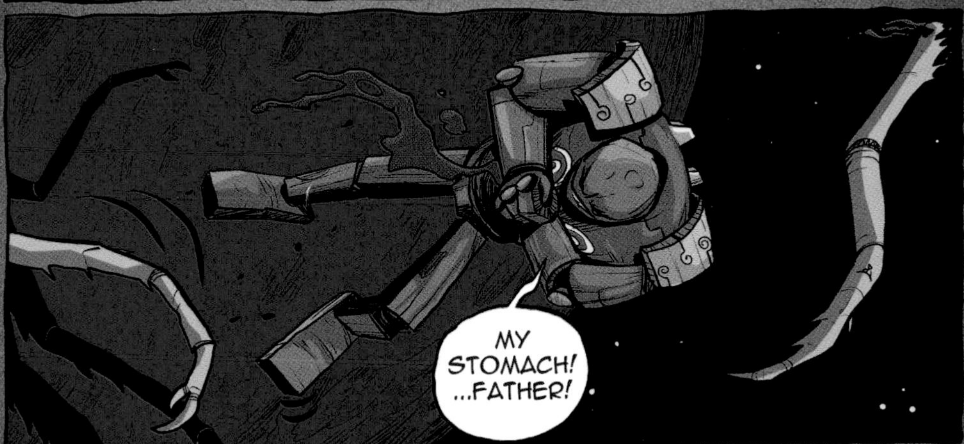
MY STOMACH! ...FATHER!

WAIT!!

GET AWAY FROM ME, YOU TRIANGLE HEAD!
DO NOT LEAVE ME!

I WILL MAKE IT WORTH YOUR WHILE!
I DON'T WANT TO HEAR ANYTHING YOU HAVE TO SAY!

I HAVE NO LOYALTY TO MY PEOPLE! IF YOU HELP--
I AM NOT GOING TO LISTEN TO YOU! MY PEOPLE KNOW THAT YOU ARE ALL LIARS!

BUT I CAN FIX YOUR SIDE! I CAN TURN ON YOUR ARMOR!
YOU... ...YOU CAN DO THAT?

YOU WILL BE THE GREATEST WARRIOR!

OKAY, BUT HURRY! I DON'T WANT MY FATHER TO SEE THAT I DISOBEYED HIM!
VVVT

I HAVE YOU NOW!

WAIT! WHAT DID YOU JUST DO? I'M TRYING TO MOVE MY ARMS AND LEGS BUT THEY DO NOT OBEY MY WISHES!
I AM IN CONTROL OF YOU NOW, PRINCE!!

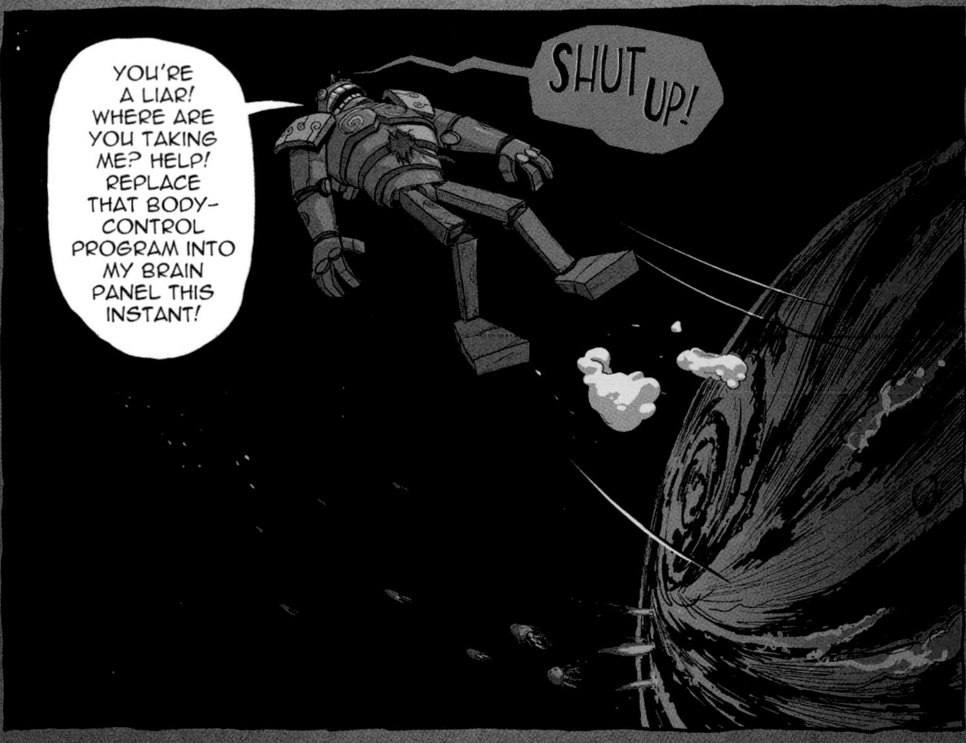
YOU'RE A LIAR! WHERE ARE YOU TAKING ME? HELP! REPLACE THAT BODY-CONTROL PROGRAM INTO MY BRAIN PANEL THIS INSTANT!
SHUT UP!

HEAR ME, SUPREME RULER! I HAVE THE PRINCE UNDER MY CONTROL!
WELL DONE...

NEWARK PUBLIC LIBRARY
121 HIGH ST
NEWARK NY 14513

WE HAVE YOUR SON!
WE HAVE TAKEN HIM TO A SECRET PLACE!
SURRENDER!

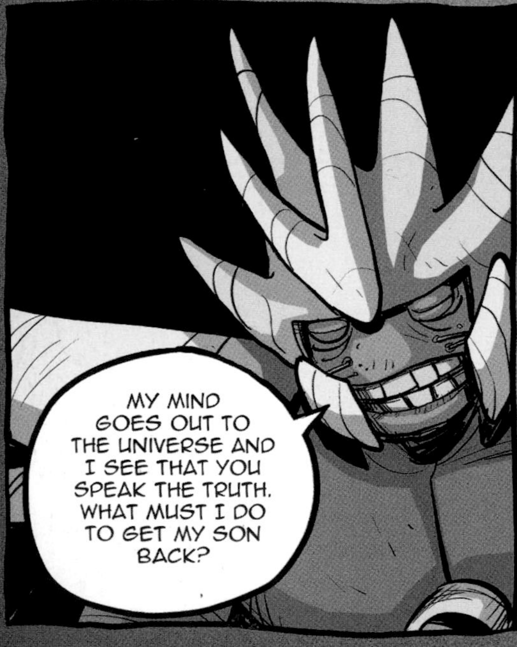
MY MIND GOES OUT TO THE UNIVERSE AND I SEE THAT YOU SPEAK THE TRUTH. WHAT MUST I DO TO GET MY SON BACK?

YOU WILL NOT GET HIM BACK, BUT HE WILL REMAIN ALIVE IN CRYO-SLEEP.

SEND WORD TO ALL GUARDIANS THAT WE MUST LEAVE THE BATTLEFIELD WITHOUT DELAY!
YES, KING.

BUT MY KING! YOU CANNOT DO THIS! IT WAS YOU WHO LIBERATED US, AND NOW YOU RETURN US TO SLAVERY?

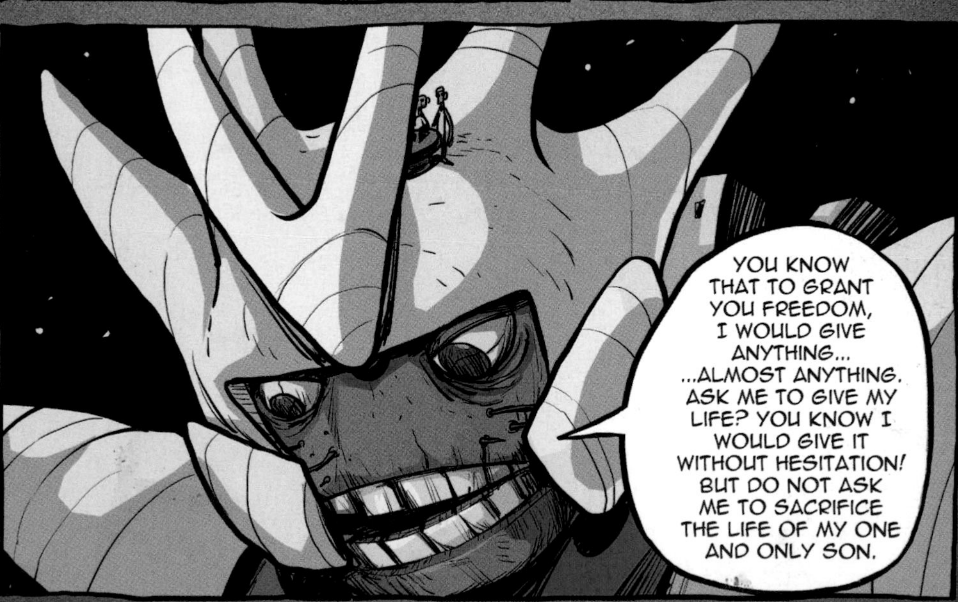
YOU KNOW THAT TO GRANT YOU FREEDOM, I WOULD GIVE ANYTHING... ...ALMOST ANYTHING. ASK ME TO GIVE MY LIFE? YOU KNOW I WOULD GIVE IT WITHOUT HESITATION! BUT DO NOT ASK ME TO SACRIFICE THE LIFE OF MY ONE AND ONLY SON.

MOTHER... ...FATHER...I AM SORRY! WILL ANYONE HEAR MY CRY FOR HELP?
NOBODY CAN HEAR YOU SCREAM OUT HERE!

NOW, YOU GO TO SLEEP!

CHONK

EARTH, A.D. 554.

CHOOM

HERE YOU WILL STAY. BUT IF YOU CAN BE SEEN, YOU CAN BE FOUND!

I ORDER YOU TO BE COVERED IN ROCK!

FOOSH
PLUNK
PLUNK
PLUNK

YOU WILL BE HIDDEN, BURIED IN FLORA TO MATCH THE PLANET!

AND IF A VISITOR SHOULD COME TO US...

...PERHAPS TO STEAL THE SOURCE OF YOUR LIFE FOR HIS OWN PEOPLE...

...HE WILL BE MET BY SOME OF THE MOST HOSTILE CREATURES IN THE UNIVERSE!

DO YOU STILL HAVE THAT ARTIFACT, REESE?
YEAH.

HERE GOES NOTHIN'!

LOGAKK TEEK!
WANNA TAKE A GUESS AT WHAT HE'S SAYING?

SOUNDS KINDA MAD!

THOOOL!! LOKVASSS!

IF HE DOESN'T WANT US TO RETURN THIS, THEN IT MUST BE A GOOD IDEA!

WE CAN HELP, TOO!

GREAT, WE GET A STANDARD-SIZED SLOT FOR A METRIC ARTIFACT!

HAXSSSSS!
AGH!

BAP
GET AWAY!

ZZZT
ZZZT

ZZZT
HOW ARE YOU DOING THIS? LET GO OF MY HAND!

URKS!
GIVE ME BACK MY BODY, JERK!
ZZT
ZZT

I CAN DO IT FOR YOU!

ZOK!

PICKLES!

EAT THIS, BUDDY!
SPLAT
KRAAAA!

CHONK

BVARRR

NOSTIKK VASK-ON!

ZIKK
ZIKK

ZIKK
ZIK

SSSSS

PICKLES...

DAD, LOOK!
I DON'T BELIEVE IT!

WAAAAAH!
BITE!

I DON'T GET IT! THAT SNAKE WAS DEAD!
...SO WAS THIS ISLAND!

CRACK

KROSH

POOM

FUMM

RUMBLE
RUMBLE

RUMBLE
RUMBLE

FUMM

KROSH

OH, DEAR! WE'RE GOING UP!
THIS ISLAND IS NOT AN ISLAND!

HROOARR

STAY AWAY FROM THE EDGE!
OKAY, DAD. BUT I'M NOT AFRAID ANY-MORE. THIS IS A GOOD GIANT!

EESTOVOK!
THE LIZARD-HEADED CREEP IS BACK!

OSKK!
EVARR!

ZZZT
ZERK!

ZZZT
ZZZZT
OCKLEX!

SNAP.

VOOOOOSSS!

KRATCHIKK AXIK-OSK-EETENOKH!

WAIT A MINUTE! I'VE SEEN THIS CREATURE BEFORE!
HE HAS BEEN COMMUNICATING WITH US ABOUT HIS PLIGHT SINCE WE FIRST ARRIVED ON THE ISLAND!
JUST THINK! HE'S FROM ANOTHER WORLD!
THEN HOW DID HE GET HERE, ON EARTH?
MAYBE HE'S A RUNAWAY.

WAAAAAAAAAAAAH
SNAP

GOOD ARM!

SPLASH

GASP

OXEKK!!

VOSK--

PLIP

CHOOM

RUMBLE
RUMBLE

BOOM

WHEEEEEEE!

THANK YOU FOR SAVING MY FAMILY!

HROAR

WOOSH

AWWW, I WANTED TO KEEP HIM! WHY DOES HE HAVE TO GO?
HE JUST WANTS TO BE WITH HIS FAMILY.

COME ON, LET'S GO HOME!

COOL VACATION, DAD! CAN WE DO SOMETHING AGAIN NEXT WEEK, TOO?
I'LL GO ANYWHERE SO LONG AS WE'RE TOGETHER.